N

TAM LIN

Retold by Susan Cooper

Illustrated by Warwick Hutton

MARGARET K. McELDERRY BOOKS
NEW YORK

COLLIER MACMILLAN CANADA
TORONTO
MAXWELL MACMILLAN INTERNATIONAL PUBLISHING GROUP
NEW YORK · OXFORD · SINGAPORE · SYDNEY

For Jack
—S.C.

ALSO BY SUSAN COOPER AND WARWICK HUTTON

The Selkie Girl
The Silver Cow: A Welsh Tale
(Margaret K. McElderry Books)

Text copyright © 1991 by Susan Cooper
Illustrations copyright © 1991 by Warwick Hutton

Margaret K. McElderry Books
Macmillan Publishing Company
866 Third Avenue
New York, New York 10022

Collier Macmillan Canada, Inc.
1200 Eglinton Avenue East
Suite 200
Don Mills, Ontario M3C 3N1

First Edition

Printed in Hong Kong

10 9 8 7 6 5 4 3 2 1

Library of Congress Cataloging-in-Publication Data

Cooper, Susan
Tam Lin/retold by Susan Cooper; illustrated by Warwick Hutton.
—1st ed.
p. cm.
Summary: A retelling of the old Scottish ballad in which a young
girl rescues the human knight Tam Lin from his bondage to the Elfin
Queen.
[1. Fairy tales. 2. Folklore—Scotland.] I. Hutton, Warwick,
ill. II. Title.
PZ8.C7926Tam 1991   398.21'09411—dc20
90-5571   CIP   AC   ISBN 0-689-50505-1

The clouds marched over the blue summer sky, and the cloud-shadows slid purple and grey across the hills of Scotland, as Margaret sat beside her window, sewing. She was not fond of sewing. She longed for adventure. But because she was the daughter of the king she was supposed to set a good, gentle example to all the other girls. Every morning they sat with her in the great tower of her father's castle, sewing, listening to the stories told by Margaret's old nurse and waiting to be married.

"The right man will come for you at the right time," the old nurse said, and she nodded her white-capped head. "For each of you."

"Pooh!" said Margaret. "I am not a flower waiting to be picked. I would rather do my own picking!"

The nurse said reprovingly, "Lady Margaret, you must have respect for the way of the world. Sit in quietness, sew a fine seam"—She looked expectantly at the other girls, waiting for them to recite the rules.

"Rub your skin with cucumber for softness," said fat Jana, the steward's daughter.

"Behave modestly with young men," said soft-voiced Alison, "as is fitting for a maid."

The old nurse nodded in approval. "And never travel the roads alone, or go near Carterhays."

"I don't see why not," Margaret said. "Carterhays is the prettiest wood in my father's kingdom. Roses grow there. We rode by it last week."

"But it's haunted!" Jana said. "The Elfin knight waits there, to trap young girls!"

"Tam Lin," said Margaret. "Yes. But have you ever seen him?"

"If once you saw him it would be the end of you," the old nurse said sharply. "No man would marry you then."

Margaret jumped up impatiently. "Marry, marry, marry! Can't you think about anything else?" She flung down her embroidery and ran out of the room.

"Where are you going?" cried the old nurse in alarm.

"To pick roses!" Margaret shouted back up the curving stairs. "At Carterhays!"

The men at arms sprang to attention as she ran out of the castle gate and over the drawbridge. Through the fields she went, hitching up her green skirts, looping up her long flying dark hair, until she came to the wood called Carterhays.

Oak and ash and thorn grew in the wood, with the moor stretching purple beyond. Once there had been houses, with gardens; the houses were long gone, but a few apple trees and flowers from the gardens remained, and red roses rambled wild up into the trees.

Margaret reached up and picked a rose. She smelled its fragrance, and smiled.

A deep voice said, "Why pick you the rose, Margaret, without asking leave of me?"

Margaret gasped, remembering the haunting of the Elfin knight Tam Lin. But the young man before her wore a country shirt and tunic, and his feet were bare. He looked most unlike a knight. He was remarkably hand-some, with blue eyes, sun-gold skin, and curling fair hair, but he was looking at her challengingly, unsmiling.

"Why should I ask leave of you?" said Margaret with spirit. "Carterhays belongs to my father the king, and I can come and go as I please. *And* pick roses."

The young man laughed suddenly. He reached up and pulled a red apple from the tree above his head. "And eat the king's apples," he said, holding it out.

Margaret bit into the crisp, juicy flesh. She smiled back at the young man, quite forgetting that apple trees do not normally bear ripe apples in June.

They spent all day together in the wood, happy with one another, until the sun dropped low in the sky and all at once the daylight was gone—and so, in a flash, was the young man with the golden skin and curly hair. Sorrowful, Margaret ran home through the glimmering twilight, and the men at arms on duty at the castle gate, to her astonishment, did not salute but dropped down on their knees. "Thank God you are back, milady!" one of them said hoarsely.

"Of course I'm back!" Margaret said, and she ran inside—where she found her father's court in total confusion, as if everyone were preparing for a great quest.

"The Lady Margaret is found!" voices cried all about, and the old nurse flung her arms round Margaret's neck.

"What a fuss!" Margaret said, as they brought her to her father the king. "I had a lovely day, I met a country boy. I'm sorry I wasn't home before dark."

Her father held her close, lovingly, but over his shoulder she could see the chamberlain glaring at her. He was a bad-tempered old knight with a grey beard.

"A lovely *day*?" said the chamberlain. "You have been gone for a week! You have been enchanted by Tam Lin, the Elfin knight, and you have disgraced us all!"

"No man will wed you now," the old nurse wept.

"I don't care," Margaret said. "If that's Tam Lin, he is bonnier than any young man in the kingdom. I don't believe he's an Elfin knight."

But she remembered the apple tree that bore apples out of season, and the sudden twilight, and she wondered.

The next day none of the other girls would speak to
her, so Margaret slipped out of the castle and ran back to
Carterhays. Through the green fields she went, hitching
up her long skirt and looping up her dark flying hair, and
when she came to the wood she picked a red rose.

A deep voice said, "Who picks the king's rose?" and Tam Lin was there, with his arms around her. Margaret looked into his blue eyes and she said, "Are you really an Elfin knight?"

"A knight, yes," Tam Lin said. "My father is the Earl of Roxburgh, on the other side of Scotland. But I am as human as yourself. When I was three years old I fell asleep one day in my father's garden and the Elfin Queen stole me away. I have lived captive in her kingdom ever since."

Margaret's eyes grew wide. "Is she very beautiful?"

"Beautiful but coldhearted," Tam Lin said. "The Elfin people have a pact with the Devil, that every seven years they will send a soul to Hell—and I think this year she has chosen me."

Margaret said in horror, "How can you escape?"

"Only with the help of a maid who loves me," Tam Lin said.

Margaret looked down at the red rose in her hand. "If I loved you, what should I do?"

Tam Lin said, "Tomorrow is Midsummer's Eve. The Elfin folk ride abroad that night, through England and through Scotland and through all the world wide. If you loved me, and wanted to save me, you should go after midnight to the holy well at Miles Cross, where two roads meet, and wait with your cloak wrapped around you and your horse blindfolded while the Elfin folk ride by. And I shall be there."

"How shall I know you?" Margaret said.

"A group of squires will ride by, but I shall not be with them. Then a group of ladies, and I shall not be with them. Then will come the highest group—of the King and Queen and their knights—and with them you will see me. Let the black horse pass, and the grey, but put out your hand to the white horse that breathes out fire. There on his back I shall be, one hand gloved and one hand bare, with a gold star in my coronet granted me because I am an earthly knight."

Margaret listened, amazed. "What should I do then?"

"Take my horse by the bridle," said Tam Lin, "and you will hear the Elfin Queen cry out: 'Tam Lin leaves me!' Do not look at her, or she will bewitch you. Look at me and take my bare hand."

"And then?"

"Then she will work her magic," he said, "and try to outwit you. In your hand I shall change my shape, and change my shape, and many a strange shape she will put on me. But you must hold fast, and you must not let me go. Remember always that I shall never hurt you, whatever I may seem to be. At the very last, you must drop what you hold into the well, and—you shall see what you shall see."

"That's all you can tell me?" she said.

"That's all I can tell you," said he.

"If I loved you," Margaret said, "I should do all those things."

Then she ran home, through the green fields, under the blue sky. In the turret room of the castle she found the old nurse reciting the rules for the conduct of maidens, and the maidens sitting meekly sewing their embroidery, waiting to be married to respectable men. Margaret looked at them, and thought of Tam Lin running, laughing, under the apple trees.

She went quietly to a chest and took out her green hooded cloak, and two soft woolen scarves, and put them in a private place. From there she went to the stables and watched the groom rubbing down her favorite dappled stallion, and when he was not looking she slipped the stable key into her pocket. Then she went off to dress for the banquet her father was giving that night to mark Midsummer's Eve.

At midnight, music and voices were loud in the castle and a full moon bright in the sky outside. Margaret wrapped herself in her green cloak, softly opened the stable door, and led out her dappled horse. Off she galloped through the midnight fields to Miles Cross, where two roads met among trees. The world was washed by silvery moonlight, without color anywhere.

She tethered her horse beside the well, and bound the two woolen scarves over his eyes and ears so that he should not be bewitched by the Elfin ride. She was just in time. Out beyond the moon-shadowed trees came the jingling of harness, and Margaret hid quickly behind a broad oak as the Elfin folk came riding, shining, down the road. It was a sight like none she had ever seen.

First came the squires, gleaming, fantastical. Their banners flew in the moonlight like great silver birds. Then came a company of ladies, beautiful as dreams, and then the glittering coach of the Elfin King and Queen, with their knights trotting on tall ghostly horses all around. Margaret peeped at the Elfin Queen, and saw a face lovelier than spring and colder than a winter wind.

Looming over her there passed a tall Elfin knight on a grey horse, then one on a black mare. Margaret heard her own horse shifting uneasily, tossing his blindfolded head. She flinched as fire leaped at her from the breath of the next horse, a great white stallion, and on his back she saw Tam Lin. Quickly she seized the horse's bridle.

From the coach, a high voice called out in grief and rage, "Tam Lin leaves me!"

The white horse reared. Margaret reached for Tam Lin's ungloved right hand, and he jumped down from his saddle—and then suddenly she was holding not the hand of a man but a handful of the thick fur of a huge snarling wolf. Its great head lunged at her, snapping sharp yellow teeth, blowing hot foul breath, but Margaret ducked, leaned away, and held fast.

The wolf leaped and howled, but she did not let him go.

She was giddy with the leaping when all at once the wolf was gone, and she was staggering in the open space beside the well, under the arching trees, with a twisting, wriggling snake in her hands. Its body slipped through her fingers, the muscles hard and smooth. Six feet of writhing snake coiled and recoiled around her, and flickering, venomous fangs darted at her from the moving head. Margaret dodged, and held fast. Around her in the wood she glimpsed a host of the Elfin folk, shadowy, watching.

The snake writhed and hissed, but she did not let him go.

Suddenly then the snake was gone, and instead she found herself holding two bars of bone—the antlers of a tall wild deer. She was high above the ground, sitting on his hard back. He tossed and twisted his head to knock her away against the branches of the trees, and the Elfin folk drew breath like the sighing of leaves in the wind. Margaret was flung up and down and sideways, but she held fast.

The deer bounded and danced, but still she did not let him go.

Then the deer was not there, and she felt a dreadful pain in her hands, and smelled the burning of her own skin, for instead she was holding a red-hot bar of iron. She swung round, seeking blindly for the well. The iron flared and smoldered and burned her, but she did not let it go. High and shrill her blindfolded horse whinnied from the tree where she had tied him, and Margaret ran to the sound and dropped the red-hot iron down into the water of the well.

There was a great hissing and spluttering, and clouds of steam billowed like mist through the moonlit clearing. Dimly through the clouds Margaret saw all the Elfin folk, knights and squires and ladies and the brilliant coach and steeds, fly up into the air like a flock of silver birds and vanish into the night. Echoing back to her through the dark sky came the high lament of the Elfin Queen, a long fading wail: "Tam Lin leaves me...."

Then light was growing in the eastern sky, and Tam Lin was climbing out of the well where Margaret had dropped the iron. His hair dripped wet and he wore no clothes; he was naked as the day he was born. She swung her mantle from her shoulders and he wrapped it around himself, and through the greyness of the night the cloth shone suddenly brilliant green, as the sun rose behind the wood and brought color back into the world.

Margaret looked down at her hands. The palms were pink and clear, with no sign of any burn at all.

Tam Lin said, "You have brought me to life again. One day we shall have a child, you and I, as naked and glad as the knight born today out of this well."

"We'll teach her to pick roses," Margaret said.

They untied the scarves that blindfolded the dappled horse, and together they rode back to the castle, through Carterhays wood and the green fields of Scotland, as the clouds marched over the blue summer sky and the cloud-shadows slid purple and grey across the hills.